The
Other Side of
Her
Mountain

By Marilyn Wright Dayton

Jill —
Here it is — a
short one with
a sample of
my almost
done next book
at the end —
Enjoy!
Marilyn

The Other Side of Her Mountain is a work of fiction. Names, characters, places and incidents are the product of the author's imagination or are used fictitiously. Any resemblance to actual events, locales, or persons, living or dead is entirely coincidental.

Published through Amazon Kindle Direct Publishing

Original Copyright © 1995

ISBN: 9798985320251

DEDICATION

I would like to dedicate this book to my family, as I always do, because they are such a huge part of my happy world. I am in a place now, retired, where I can release all of those stories that have been in my head. And with the encouragement of my family and friends, this, my eighth book, is here.

I have always loved reading. I have always loved writing. I wrote several short stories and books in the mid-1990s, that had to wait almost 30 years before I pulled them out of the box, once the pandemic began.

Here is one of them.

Marilyn
AUTHOR

THE OTHER SIDE OF HER MOUNTAIN

PROLOGUE

Many of us have lived through dark and unhappy days. And those who are lucky get to see the light at the end of those times. During one of my unhappy times, I found that writing a story helped me, like therapy. And so I wrote *"The Healing",* a short fictional story included in my book **"Beyond."**

When I read that story again a couple of years later, I had found myself in another philosophical, sad place. So, I decided to take the idea from "*The Healing*" and expand on it.

This is the result. It has been in a storage box for almost 30 years. Since I am more of a happy soul these days, I have found myself a writer of several published books. So, why not turn this one into a book too?

I no longer write like this story. Today, my writing has more lightness to it. This is a deep, dark story of a ten-year-old girl who finds the courage to climb out of the darkness and find the other side of her mountain.

-    Originally written in 1995.

Marilyn
AUTHOR

THE OTHER SIDE OF HER MOUNTAIN

AUNT LIBBY

My Aunt Libby died last week, Monday or Tuesday. I don't know which. In her will, she asked me to make her a promise, not because I knew her and loved her, but because there was no one else.

She was a stranger to me. I knew as much about her as she thought I needed to know, as much as anyone needed to know. My father, her brother, had told me she was an enigma. A rather famous one. She had lived for her work, nothing and no one else. Except perhaps for her loving companion, with whom she traveled a great deal the second half of her life. She seemed to intimate that there were family secrets buried deep within Libby's silence.

That is all I knew. Whenever our paths had crossed, perhaps five or six times in my life, she would barely nod to me. She knew of my longing to be a successful writer, as she had been, yet she never dignified that truth until now.

She left me her memoirs. I looked at her sheaf of papers and wondered, '*Why do people read this stuff? What are they supposed to find here in the memories of someone once proclaimed a famous writer? Solace? Reassurance? Something from someone else's life that they can connect to?*'

I held the thick grouping of handwritten pages and wondered whether they were full of joy or heartache. I had always hated reading about someone else's sorrows, founded in pain and loss, forming an analogous national literature. You see, I connect with Charles J. Sykes, who complains that the United States society has "*degenerated into a community of insistent sufferers,*" that "*our National Anthem has become a whine.*"

But I honor promises. She bequeathed that I ensure her journal, her story, be published. And so, I began to read it. And I found I was wrong – this is not a story of self-pity, simply not a motive adequate enough for her to expend precious effort.

This was a woman who became famous, whose fictional writing had themes that made people look inward, contemplating their very existence. She had such power, such strength, and you could feel it in the millions of words she wrote.

Her own story is one of survival as a child, her painfully personal story of her journey to self-acceptance and self-value. After reading her story, I wish she had written more about her life as a writer and as a *'woman of difference.'*

This is but one story where she shares the secret she held dear all her life. It's the beginning of a love story – *'a love of self story'*. This story tells of how she was let to a new life and the beginnings of her passion for writing. It is a compelling story. Her memoir has changed my life. Perhaps this particular story of an event that changed her life may also change yours.

And so, I share it with you. As promised. - *Emma*

UNHAPPY, CRUMPLED PAPER

I see myself surrounded by crumpled bits of paper. Although it is October, the weather is sweltering, the day radiantly lit with sunshine. I sit outside and write this, surrounded by the color and smells of strong weeds that stifle my senses. I sit upon a piece of shaded earth, beside a shallow but steadily trickling stream. I am alone with nature, and my memories. A perfect setting to remember and write.

This hard ground is softened only by colorful but fading leaves, turning from their smooth, silky flexibility to a dry crunching-sort of material, left on the ground for the world to tread upon and turn to dust.

This is my happiness. This is my belonging, the only kind of real union I have ever wanted or needed. Mother Nature knows how to give and provide comfort and security to those who love her. To those who abuse her, she offers damage and pain. She and I are so much alike – oh, how we long to be left alone – just to be what we are meant to be. I could dissolve right now and become one with her, and I would feel complete.

I look upward and see my life as it formed. But now my sky is so black with storm clouds that I can see above me the changing scenes of my life as soft blurs in the feathery, troubled motion.

I am an artist and I have searched and worked to achieve truth in my work. At least I feel I have, and I feel the union of the great forces of anger, deceit, weakness, and cruelty I have been dealt in life. I have never allowed myself to feel a normal, romantic kind of love, it was never there for me. But instead of the obvious emptiness that should present itself, there has been a strength of

9

purpose and security within myself. Indeed, is that not a kind of love? It is simply another shape above me that covers the heavens.

My life has been as this collection of dark clouds so far above me; while I have lived it, not as an observer of my own life, but of others as though they were a part of my own essence. All the while, my skies have changed, my roots have been firm and deep within the earth, strong and growing. Now, at the end, I recap it all, and my life comes pouring out of me, running back into the ground.

I never thought before of writing an autobiography, yet the many fictional stories I have written have been more or less about me. Writers are always present in their work, however thinly disguised. But I ask myself, *'Who would want to read about me?'* I always felt the fiction I wrote was like art, transforming the world. Nowhere is the power of art more evident than when applied to the unpromising material of the everyday. I may not always be able to control my autobiographical impulses, but there is a measure of control over the way I reveal my secrets.

The impulse for someone of a writerly persuasion is not to bemoan catastrophes or some other life-changing happenstance, but to remark of it in detail. The process of making sense of a flood of random data can produce an impression of control, which could help save one's sanity, but not necessarily serve one's own or anyone else's life.

These therapeutic results provide ample reason for keeping a personal journal, but certainly not for transforming intimate experience into public artifact. There is nothing, I feel, exceptional about my life, yet I feel a compulsion to share.

Success in my writing has always been, to me, when someone reads it, and it becomes a part of their history, where it changes their dreams, their lives, even a little. It's an enormous rather humbling experience to reach into your intellect, into your dreams, your own knowledge, and hand it to other people. The response you receive from those people gives you the energy and courage to write again and share it again. Over and over...

It was not until now, as memoir and the whole genre of creative nonfiction begins to flower, that the stories from my life that I'd tried to disguise and romanticize in fiction come exploding, honestly and urgently onto the page.

Today, perhaps the world is ready for this journal. As a writer, a teacher, a reader myself, I see how today's readers are hungering for truth in the first person. Perhaps because we live in an age where it is now commonly felt that our pollical leaders are liars and thieves. People are asking for historic reality from '*real people*' whose solitary landscapes and single voices have a power that illuminates the larger humanity we all share...which makes the strange familiar and the familiar strange.

But I can't divorce myself by intellect from any experiences I've had – my personal encounter with the truth. And my truth is that my '*road of life*' led to my breaking one of society's taboos. I don't condemn '*society*' for trying to dictate my life, I have certainly never been in danger of obeying any of the rules anyway. Perhaps that is why my writing has always been so popular throughout my career – I was a rebel but never condemned that which I rebelled from.

All else, I kept private until now. But now, as I near the end, I need you to enter my life and endure it with me. It's the only way I can reconnect myself – now so utterly transformed by events unlike any I've experienced as to seem a stranger even to myself – to the human community. A community that would have condemned me, had they known, to obscurity, away from fame and societal respect.

They say that we are what we have done – that our life experiences have defined who we are. It doesn't matter that much, does it, who we are at the very end? Doesn't it mean more to the world, who we were as we developed, lived and contributed along the way?

As the French historian Michelet expressed it:

"The end is nothing,
The road is all."

~ *Libby*

THE BEGINNING

To share private thoughts is to find a common bond with the receiver and with that comes forgiveness, and with forgiveness comes love and understanding. I stepped into life with ardor, ignorant and alone.

When I was born in 1920, the world was coming up out of turmoil, seeming not to notice me. But my father noticed. My father, who awaited another son to help him in his farming profession.

My first few years of life have been erased, blotted out from my mind. My first real memory is my banishment to a closet when I was five. No light, no food, very little air. I would find myself there often, the first decade of my life, hiding from my violent father, ignored by my unapproachable mother.

My home was not really a home – I felt I never really belonged, as if I had been exiled while still living there. I have to acknowledge that the vanishing of thoughts that had made up the world of my early childhood somehow has created a void in me, as if half of my guts had been removed, yet somehow I survived.

Sometimes we select only the memories of our childhood that made our hearts happy, but alas, I had none of these. The only view of my first decade of life that excited me was not being there. I chose not to dwell upon the furious sounds of quarrels and insults, the stinging slaps of my father's oversized farm hands, and the quiet, lonely pain of the locked closet.

The best story I know I was afraid to tell. Afraid lest it be misunderstood. I thought many times that my early life with them was the family secret. If I described my brittle, caustic father, my jumpy brother, my reclusive mother, you could probably see how all their lives have been shaped by me, and how my life has been shaped by them.

It isn't an easy story to tell because it doesn't have a happy, fairy-talish end. Today it exists for me AS a story, rather than my past life. But the story that I will sketch, despite a certain heartsick guilt, matters to me. I cannot fall under the illusion that because I remember this story from so long ago, I understand it, why it happened and how it affected us all.

The most difficult lives to write about, and the ones that draw us most are full of mystery and familiarity. They seem to be the ones where there are the greatest chance people will read it and, despite different names and places, recognize themselves or someone they know.

My father, a man with a stiff upper body like a door, used to sit at the table mutely reading a newspaper, seemingly oblivious of his children, as we sat silently at the same table. My father seemed a person bereft of love, instead a red, bloated face, a gargoyle of itself, pulling my ear between viselike fingers, as he hatefully pushed and pulled me into the closet, into the silent, hateful darkness. His voice booming through the locked door, "*I don't know what I have done to you that you never listen to me.*"

The comment struck me as so naïve. Confusion smothered my feelings about him, and his true emotion remained invisible to me. Which one of us was wrong and which was wronged? I have tried to access something living in me, living incognito, perhaps only half-formed as I was at that age. I feared his action proved I had no worth. That I was nothing.

Our sword in the stone grows straight down from our parents. All of our lives we seek confirmation from them, wanting their solidity and approval.

Sometimes when I dream of my childhood, my family, I

awaken with the feeling I can't go on. Being so close to them again puts me in touch with my deep natural sense of horror. A writer's work requires unburying events and emotions which have been suppressed. I feared that my childhood was the spark that propelled my work - if I faced my past and dealt with it psychologically, would I lose that spark? Was my writing the release of all that horror I suppressed? Or was it all the emotions I suppressed while working actually going into my creations? Perhaps I ask this in search not for objective truth but for emotional truth.

The dysfunction in our house was obvious, in a way that there was no need to discuss it. It was what one could not for a moment forget. By not discussing it, though, it was as if one must see our parents but not see them. We saw them and didn't see them…we spoke to them and didn't speak to them…we loved them for who they were and we refused to acknowledge who they were. Are all secrets this obvious?

My mother did the cooking and cleaning. Otherwise, she was in bed, '*with a headache*'. I don't remember her ever saying much to me except "*You mind your father.*" She never voiced an opinion. She hugged my brother, but never touched me. It was as if I wasn't really hers, that I didn't belong. In the good times, I would be running free on the land, chasing clouds, animals, anything. Or talking quietly with my brother, my only friend. He taught me to bathe, to dress, to eat, to brush my teeth, to do some farm chores. He was the only one I could relate to, either in our family or in our small town.

Our father was a farmer, busy all day long. By the time he would notice me, he was usually out of patience, overtired and frustrated by something. Since my brother was older and could help him work the farm, I was, by comparison, pretty useless to him. And I was, by nature, pretty sassy. So, it was only natural that he'd take out his frustrations on me – either with his hand, his belt, or by banishment to the closet.

THE OTHER SIDE OF HER MOUNTAIN

I never asked God for help. I didn't believe in Him. What I did was invent an imaginary friend, someone to spend the hours with in that closet. His name was Boyd Chance. He was ageless, that was not important. What was important to me was he was free to do what he wanted, and he wanted to be a veterinarian because, like me, he loved animals of all kinds. They were kinder to you than people were. And showed appreciation and love.

I recognize now that Boyd was the other side of me. The same intelligence, the same personality, all the same, except he was a male. And I know that the part of me that invented him was the same part that wanted a hug from my mother, and to be able to work alongside my father. Boyd was always by my side, until a tragedy freed me soon after my tenth birthday.

THE BIG SEPARATION

My brother was four years older. He held the important position of being my one and only lifeline to this world. Out of his need to survive, he was contrite to our parents and to everyone else. But he seemed to be able to feel my rebellious feelings, perhaps felt encouraged, through me, to live them. He understood me and accepted me as I was, without encouraging me to change.

I saw him as I now see the world – as contrast. Contrast between artist and society, ideas and realities, desire and necessity, and above all, a soul divided against itself. He was a shallow figure, his lack of convictions was a weakness to me. His matter-of-fact acceptance of life was unacceptable and hard for me to comprehend.

Our brother-sister relationship was emotion VS intellectualism. In that first decade of my life, I recognized parts of him inside myself, conceding there was a duality in my nature. I wanted to be strong, not like him. I refused to cling to weakness as he did, treating that sad element of his own nature as more precious than strength.

He was the prime example set before me of other children, of brains wired to think along the path of least resistance, the most worn path. I was contrast – a child taught not to touch the flame, then wanting to touch it.

And so, on the day of the tragedy, I found myself again in the closet. It always felt as if I sat in the darkened corner for days rather than hours. I couldn't leave this strange refuge because the chains that locked me in were my father's loud voice and insistent, grave stare. I would call out in my mind to my silent jailer for release and receive no answer.

Staring at the lone, faint slit of light that reminded me there was still a world outside this cell, I wondered if the door was truly locked this time. My mind shouted at me to try the knob, but my fears overrode such action. If found making such an attempt at unsanctioned release, my ten-year-old hide would be whipped. Fear, always a menace in my short-lived past, had triumphed again. And so, I waited for my jailer to reappear.

The house was still except for a few dishes clanging in the kitchen, where my brother was preparing himself lunch. Hours earlier, our parents had left on an errand, and I felt surprised that there were no signs of a reappearance by now.

My stomach felt compelled to interrupt the quiet, and I wondered if my brother would chance sneaking me some food. But fear of our father seemed as much a part of his life as mine, and I attempted to resettle my body, mentally countermanding the hunger pangs.

I heard a car approach the house and my body froze in response, tightening my muscles into rubber bands stretched to their maximum capacity. But the voices were strange ones, not my parents. The tension did not lessen in my body, because other members of our small community saw us as 'outsiders'.

The orbiting earth and its atmosphere are the real fact, and each man's existence goes on within and beneath it, caught up in his own little world. Sometimes they work *en masse*, as in a small community, and grow bigotry as if it were a crop they watched from seed to harvest. And it feeds their egos, so they reseed and continue to grow it, until their little world is so full of jealousy and envy and unhappiness, they try to close their invisible doors to outsiders. No one else is welcome in their area of existence.

Their lives go on – made up of evasions and negations, fed by their increasing appetite for gossip. Every individual's activity is bridled by caution, suspicion, pointing the finger elsewhere, as if the town were inhabited by bloodsuckers, creeping quietly about in the dark.

This small community of my first decade represented *'the world'*, offering only danger to me. I didn't believe in these people, this town, God, or even my own parents, who had banished and punished me. I believed in nature, animals and myself.

Each time life, or someone, disappoints you, it is painful. And you change – a little. It's like a little reminder stays with you, like a little thorn stuck in your brain. And it makes you a little more careful the next time. It's part of a process called maturing.

My lessons in maturity advanced a great deal that day. I heard approaching feet, and my brother opened the closet door, calling me out in hushed tones. His features drew themselves into what might have been a smile under other circumstances. All he said immediately was, *"You're free now."* And he walked away.

The strangers met us in the kitchen, with frowning faces, and few words. *"Your parents are dead. We've contacted your grandparents, and you will go live with them."*

My first decade of life was bleak and weary, as Winter. Winters could sometimes seem a savage punishment to use humans for loving the loveliness of Summer. But yet, in my young life, I had not yet experienced *'Summer'*, only all-existent Winter. As if cold winds had stripped away all the leafy screens that hide the horizon, all I could see was the continuation of bleakness as far as my eyes could see. In Winter, the inside of warmer houses should draw families close together. The members of our family were close only in body, not spirit, and certainly not emotion. Any conversation had only been ones of compliance. Just like a perpetual Winter, there had been a hunger inside of me for color to hide the bleakness. The colors of Spring.

Winter hung on too long here, in my parent's house. Their lives had been stale and shabby, old and sullen. And before they died, my snows had grown increasingly gray and mournful-looking.

THE OTHER SIDE OF HER MOUNTAIN

Leaving that house gave me the opportunity to discover Spring, where the world would slowly come alive for me.

ON THE ROAD

After my parents died, I became separated from that cruel, painful world and baffled by the changes that living with my grandparents suddenly presented. Then girl, grandparents, and new landscape had fates joined inextricably, like the threads of a tapestry. My old tapestry – the landscape of suffering had been transformed into one of hope and humaneness.

James Joyce said that one has not lived unless one has conceived of life as a tragedy. My first ten years were, but I must make some distinction between what tragedy exacts and depression produces in my case, perhaps spawning an industry of literary knitting?

My first literary indications began on the ride to my grandparents. We rode on a railway train, our first time. Although he was fourteen, my brother's experience of the world was not much wider than mine. Neither of us had been outside the invisible walls of the small farming community where we had both been born. Neither set of grandparents had ever traveled to see us. So, I had no mental picture of our material grandparents, the ones we were going to live with. They must have been unable to come to us, we rode the train without escort.

Initially, the train was huge, feeling like cold, sterile metal under my inspecting fingers, and was quite noisy as well as strange-smelling. But after the first few miles passed beneath the wheels, the friendly passenger conductor took my brother and I under his wing. He knew much about the countryside we were traveling through and shared interesting stories and traveling insights with us. He seemed like such an experienced and worldly man who had been everywhere.

His uniform made him a rather stately figure. His confident enthusiasm calmed us, as we were two inexperienced travelers unsure of the world outside. The scenery as well as time moved rather swiftly, and we soon arrived at our destination.

This friendly stranger had enthralled me, leading me to make myself a promise, a vow. I would study and travel and become a storyteller, making children like myself happier.

My heart pounded fast and heavy in my child's chest as I looked out the window at what would be our new home. The evening darkness swallowed all the scenery but for two men running about with lanterns. At first, it seemed an enlarged version of my closet – full of cold emptiness.

A chill passed through me, and I felt that somehow things wouldn't be that different, at least for me. From all that I had read, I surmised that people were generally the same wherever you went. And that meant that anyone who fancied themselves uncommon would be set aside from the rest, unwelcomed and ignored except for an occasional stare, rude comment, or finger-pointing. I sighed deeply, aloud, along with the sounds of the tired panting of the engine after such a long run. The conductor collected us, and pulled us to the train's exit, where we stood hugging close our meager belongings.

A man with a lantern approached us talking, shouting, exclaiming. We were to follow him, according to our temporary friend, the conductor. He gave us each a pat on the back and off we moved. Inside the train station, there were many people, some speaking strange sounds. I now realize this was the first time I had actually heard a foreign language being spoken.

I heard more shouts that seemed to be coming nearer, and realized a round, flushed, old woman was going to run us over.

But she stopped, smiling and waving her arms, *"My precious babies!"* And quickly enveloped my brother and me into her wide embrace. At first, I was concerned, as I found it hard to breathe. And then I realized that this was what it was like to be hugged, surrounded by soft warmth, and I liked it.

Grandfather, a quick and wiry man, grimaced and gestured angrily for her to release us so we could begin the last part of our journey. He rushed us all off to find their truck.

There were enough lights in the streets that we were able to view our new town, full of tall buildings. All I saw was these dark and eerie-looking buildings, but I was not really looking at them. My mind was. My heart searched in vain for fences, creeks and trees, hills and fields. The road was rough, and the bumps were easily felt by our tired, aching bodies. I found myself turning my head away so no one could see, and for the first time since my parents had died, I could feel warm tears on my cool cheeks.

I didn't cry because I had lost my parents, or from aching so much; I cried because I couldn't see my beloved countryside. I felt the loss of the wild animals I had watched, the farm animals I had cared for, the fields I loved to run in, the many smells of the country. I felt like my world was left behind, that my brother and I had gone over the edge, banished away from the sights and sounds we knew so well. I felt that this was more punishment, being doled out especially to me, because I had been so difficult. And I cried myself into an exhausted, dreamless sleep.

MY NEW WORLD

My first morning in my new world, I woke up to familiar sounds, confusing my mind. The room I lay in was new, but those sounds – chicken cackling, pigs snorting, dogs barking, cows in the distance – weren't new. I snuck to the window, almost afraid to find it was just a dream, that instead of fields and clover, there would be those dark, tall buildings and dirty, bumpy roads from the previous night.

I felt my heart leap as I saw my beloved countryside spread before my eyes staring from my bedroom window. Everything I cared about was there, fields and flowers, fertile farmland, and animals. My grandparents' farmhouse stood in the midst of a great meadow which sloped toward a distant brook. The fields of wheat and rye were bordered by neat precise rows of cornstalks. It was a green world that I saw under the light of the rising sun. And I felt the day was fine, rather than really seeing it. My eyes were fixed on a distant memory – I had brought all of the good things from my life with me.

My grandmother, by the light of early day, was cheerful and supportive, wishing only that I wasn't so inclined *"to take such a sad view of life."* It was hard to smile when you had never been taught.

After breakfast, she took my hand and led me outside, urging me to explore my new world. The meadows that led to the brook's edge were the greenest in all the world because as I look back, they were the meadows of long ago, and the flowers that grow there are the freshest and sweetest smelling because that first morning, a child gathered them, and once again I am surrounded by the beauty of that vanished early Autumn.

My grandmother and I sat quietly beside the brook, holding our sweet-smelling bouquets, calmed and soothed by the brook, so sluggish in its movements as to be in slow motion.

My grandmother began to tell me about her daughter, my mother, about how she had been at my age. It seemed, from her recanted memories, my mother had been a quiet, contemplative and always unhappy young person for some reason. In sad tones, she turned to look at me with puzzlement in her eyes, "*You know, it's a queer thing. Some people haven't much, but they like what they have. There are other people who have everything and don't like anything. Your mother didn't have much, didn't seem to know what she wanted, so didn't know what to dream of, to hope for. I fear she died still unhappy.*"

Her voice sank so low and was sometimes so charged with feeling that at times I almost thought she had forgotten my presence and was remembering aloud to herself. As she talked, I hid myself in the tall grasses, where the droppings of a leaf or the whistle of a bird was the only incident. I didn't really want to hear of my mother's selfishness and confusion. She was no longer a part of my life, if she had ever really been.

I absorbed myself in surveying my new surroundings, enveloping myself in Mother Nature's beauty. On every side of the magical meadow and brook were ragged mountains with wide, barren wounds where timber had been ruthlessly torn away. I saw these gulches in the wild countryside as wounds in the earth, and tears slowly began as I felt for her pain.

My grandmother mistakenly thought I was crying for my lost mother and cradled me in her arms where we silently mourned together on that grassy bank by the water's edge. The long, rank grass, thick and soft and falling in billows, made a comfortable bed for sharing memories and feelings. The bank was

25

grown up with trees, which leaned protectively over the brook and us.

There was a hush, a tragic submission, and the water trickled slowly, flowing soundlessly as my grandmother continued to talk of long-ago days. The wind was a little more than a sighing in the heavy grasses.

I lay in her arms thinking of my own life and my now distant memories, and this smallest of rivers seemed to carry them away, providing some kind of small healing within me. As I lay there, lost with her in the unconscious present, the wind began to rise, stirring the light foliage above our heads and bringing the woody odor of nearby wild roses that overran one edge of the meadow.

The experiences she shared with me seemed to rent her in pieces, as I felt such same stirring in the obvious abuse of my beloved countryside. It was like the feeling artists know when they finally achieve truth in their work. The feeling of union with some great force, of purpose and security, of being glad we lived. For the first time, I felt the pull of blood and kindred, and felt beating within me things that had not begun with me. It was as if the earth under my body had grasped me and was pouring its essence into me.

BEYOND THE MOUNTAIN

When I try to recall those first few weeks with my grandparents, I remember my grandmother mostly. She was not much taller than I was even then, at ten years old. She was round and soft, always hugging my brother and I to her ample bosom. Her hair was almost purely white. She once told me it had been so since she was thirty. She loved flowering plants and always wore a housedress shouting of small violets or bright rosebuds. Her domain was the kitchen, so she always wore a full apron that mostly covered her dresses. I can still close my eyes and smell the gingerbread baking.

Where my grandfather was fairly quiet and wore a furrowed brow in his constant state of worry, she wore a smile and laughed a lot. She would often wear a look with an attitude of attention with her head slightly cocked. As I look back on it, I believe her thoughts would drift away then, to some other space in time.

There seemed no pressure there, but we were each allowed our own time and space, and it was a period of contentment for me. While my brother helped Grandfather in the fields of corn and wheat, Grandmother and I tended the animals and garden. It was my first inkling of what a normal family life was like. The stark contrast of my first ten years was not repeated again. There was no real need for me to resurrect my earlier imaginary friend, nor my dreams of being far away from my current situation, for it was no longer full of pain.

But my rebellious attitude still grew strong in me. Today,

you would call me a true nonconformist. My first, rough attempts at writing occurred during this time, a journal of observations. I always carried it with me to the edge of the cornfield in early morning and reflected on the days as I sat on an old tree stump along the pathway. I kept the journal hidden deep under my mattress where no one would find it. It was only for my eyes. My writings were not meant for the world to read, yet.

Grandmother's garden was a wonder, potatoes buried beneath their withering green plantings, fat, yellow pumpkins that lay unprotected by their withering vines, juicy raspberries and blackberries, so tempting that less than half of those picked ever made it to the house. My brother, who rarely ventured in the garden, loved the green pole beans, picked fresh from their bushy plants. A strange choice, they tasted so bitter uncooked.

I remember standing in the garden, my face shaded by one of Grandmother's bonnets, looking out across the cornfields thinking that I could walk straight through those fields and over the edge of the world, which could not be far away. The light air that touched my cheeks told me that the world ended here, only the ground and sun and sky were left. And if I walked a little further, there would be only sun and sky, and I could float off into them, like the curious black crows that watched me, occasionally sailing over our heads making slow shadows on the ground.

It was a friendly garden. There was a ground hog that lived in a hole in a mound behind the pumpkins. He was furry brown and fat like a big possum. He liked to come out once in a while to sit and sniff the air. He didn't seem to mind that I was so close by and would sometimes watch Grandmother and I work in the garden.

I used to wonder at such a creature, wanting to join him in his state of contented lightness. I would sit nearby, leaning back against a warm, yellowing pumpkin, eating berries, and watch his world come alive. Giant grasshoppers would do acrobatic feats among the dried vines. The breezes would gently rock the tall grasses and corn stalks while squirrels scurried up and down the straight aisles close by. The earth was warm under me, and still feeling warm as it crumbled and fell through my fingers. I would watch black ants scurry by in squadrons around me, that somehow knew to leave me untouched. I became like them all, creatures at one with the earth and the warm air; and wondered if that was what it was like to die, to become part of something so complete. And that became my happiness, to be dissolved into something complete and great.

My grandfather had a gift of simple and moving expression. Because he talked so little, his words had a peculiar force; they were not worn dull from constant use. His face had a look of weariness and pleasure, like that of sick people when they felt relief from pain. When his deep-set eyes rested on me, I felt as if he were looking far ahead into the future for me, down the road I would have to travel.

I had arrived at my new home with something akin to survival starvation, without succumbing to want because I was never aware of it. I felt I could never be really as hungry for food or friendship as I was in that first decade of my life.

In my new home, the city and school lessons taught me whatever was needful for me to know. Little by little, my agony of ignorance alleviated, and my spontaneity was born, and life quickened in me a sense of the universal unfairness of things, training my eye and ear to the subtleties of the thousand types of atmospheres. I became clearer of vision, and the ease of writing it all in my daily journal came close to overwhelming me with the rush of it.

At last, I was able to go beyond the mountain. It meant more than just passing over land. On one side of that mountain, where I lived my first decade of life, was hidden horrible things. Now I could leave them there, back where they were lived, beyond the mountains and in my past. The valley under that mountain is like a burned-out volcano, its day is over. I was enroute to a new beginning, where the doings of the real world go on.

- THE END -

ABOUT THE AUTHOR

Marilyn Wright Dayton has been writing all her life, from the time she could hold a pencil. Her life and career focused on the world of advertising in many roles. She was one of the originators of some of the more unique marketing vehicles in the nation over the years.

As an innovator in the new world of women and leadership, she has proven to create peak performances in startups, small businesses and non-profits. From the beginning of her career at the age of 12 as a radio quiz kid, she has been both in front of the camera and behind the camera as a fashion model, radio and TV show host and program producer. She holds degrees in marketing and business as well as in journalism. Over the past several decades, she has also been a newspaper reporter, creative writer, ad director, entrepreneur, consultant, trainer/coach and an authority in the areas of creative marketing and top-notch business performance.

Through those years, her first loves have continued to be creative writing and art. She brings that to her research for her family's genealogy book *"Our Roots Run Deep",* available on Amazon. Her published books of short stories are also available on Amazon. She has published several novels and is at work on several more planned over the next few years. See some of them on the last few pages here.

Marilyn is now retired from the business world and makes her home with her family in Mystic, CT.

www.MarilynDayton.com
maredayt@yahoo.com

A Look Inside "A Matter of Time" Guy Davis Mystery Series Book 1

CHAPTER 1

I DON'T WANT TO BE HERE

He was where he had to be. Not where he wanted to be. And, in the middle of the night, Homicide Detective Guy Davis turned off his car and leaned back in his seat. It was raining, and he felt like he was wrapped up in a metal cocoon, isolated from everybody and everything. He had been called out on another homicide, to another city. But he didn't feel ready yet. It seemed like after 17 years as a cop, seeing everything there was to see, you'd get used to it. Yet, it was the kind of work he enjoyed – the challenges, and the way each case was always different. Different, but still the same. Someone was dead. He had to mentally get himself ready to see another person dead. So, he closed his eyes, and hummed quietly to himself.

He had to clear his mind. Clear his green-eyed redhead out of his mind. She was with him every day. He could see her during the day and in his dreams every night. Jesus! He had to pull himself together.

All right. Get out of the car and get in there. Take your notebook and pen. He reached over to his glove compartment, noticed the small flask of whiskey, deciding it would help relax him and warm him up. It was the day after Easter Sunday and it was damp and cold in Detroit. He felt sure it was the same in New York City, where he served on the force. He pulled down a warm, bitter swig, took a deep breath and moved to get out of the car.

Wait, his hand fell from the door handle. Why was he here again? Why did his Chief send him all the way from New York City to Detroit? He pulled another swig to help clear his brain from the fog that had developed during the long drive.

Oh, yeah. There was a murder several days ago here. The Police Chief here was a friend with his NYC Chief and asked for a profiler to help with the case. His Chief thought it would be good for Guy, to get away for a while, focus on a case in a new territory. Maybe it would help him forget.

There she was again. Flashing green eyes, that went so well with her flashing smile, throwing back her long red hair. Damn!

He moved out of the car and went into the station.

There was a lot of noise inside, people complaining who appeared poorly dressed and dirty, yelling at the poor cop standing behind the front desk. Other cops milling around, all talking at the same time. He shook his head, and moved to the left down a hallway, sure he could figure out how to find the Chief.

Then he heard a big, booming voice, reeming out one of the cops who had apparently missed something on a case, and a door being slammed. He followed the noise. He found the closed door, opened it and smiled at the big man behind the desk.

"Who the Hell are you?" His voice fit his large body.

"I'm Guy Davis, from New York. You needed a profiler? So, here I am."

"Well, you look like shit!"

"Long trip. I could take time to get cleaned up, check into a

local motel, and then come back."

"No…no. Sit down. We have a lot of work to do. You'll just get rumpled up more anyway." A look of acceptance came over the large Police Chief. Then a hint of a smile. *"Let me get you caught up with the highlights, then take a long look at this file,"* which he tossed over to Davis.

"Victim is a middle-aged female, professor at the University. She was stabbed, then pushed down the stairs at the house she shared with her husband, who is several years younger than she. He supposedly had gotten home after it all happened and found her. But he is just not shook up enough about it, you know? Front door was left ajar (had had come in through the garage door into the kitchen), and there were bloody footprints leading to the front door. But, of course, he had messed them up, walking all over them. He said intruder. We think him but can't prove it. Second dead wife for him, both with large life insurance payouts."

"Sounds like an easy case to me," Guy reacted.

"The guy is the Mayor."

"Oh, I see."

The door to the Chief's office opened and a cop in plain clothes stuck his head in. *"Got a murder, new one. I need a partner, and everyone is out on a call. Who are you?"* as he looked down at Guy.

"Okay, this is your temporary partner, Guy Davis, Detective and Profiler from NYC." He looked over at Guy, *"Good way to get your feet wet, literally. Why don't you go along and help out on this one. And we can meet on the other case when you get back. Or in the morning if you are late."* And he proceeded to pick up the phone to make a call, ignoring Guy.

Guy figured he just got an assignment, stood and walked

back out the office door. He offered his hand, introducing himself. *"Yup, I'm Officer Jack Watkins. Let's get going. You got wheels?"*

Guy nodded and they headed to his car. He hoped that the flask was back in the glove compartment. He didn't want to give the wrong first impression. Even if it might be the correct one.

CHAPTER 2

DEAD GUY

He never parked right at the scene. He liked to leave his car a block or two away. That way he could check out the neighborhood, see who was standing around outside, just out of sight of the cops, waiting. Sometimes he would see someone hanging around outside, just close enough, who was either involved or knew something. He could mentally take a picture of their face and clothes, for use later. Having almost total recall helped immensely. He forgot nothing. He could even remember a page number on a report, and what was on that page. Weird. But he was grateful for that small gift. It sometimes made the difference in his work.

He never worried about his car, even in the worst of neighborhoods. It was just a tin-can shell, rusty, almost a non-color from the years. But he had an engine in that shell that could pretty much beat any race car on any road. That came in handy, too.

He got a funny look from Watkins, who was wise enough to keep his mouth closed. He must have figured parking so far from the scene was because his new temporary partner was from out of town. Smart move, as Guy wasn't in the mood to be questioned.

The street around the victim's building was disappointing. Nobody outside, but the patrol cars and some cops hanging around, waiting to be told what to do next. Of course, the rain didn't help. He could be missing someone who was trying to stay dry, hanging around in a doorway somewhere, still able to see the action at the front door, but hidden from sight.

"Hey, Watkins, what did he pull you away from this time?" One of the cops was waiting for them at the front door. *"You know you're late, as usual. Wylie is ranting and raving up there, waiting for you. Better hurry up."* Then he noticed Guy. *"And who are you?"*

Watkins looked over at Guy, *"Long story, I'm sure. He's on special assignment or something. Davis, meet Mac. Mac, meet Davis."*

Being a trained profiler means that you can learn to read people fairly quickly and pretty well. Guy could size up Mac, a guy who liked to give people a hard time. That was how you found out what people were really like. So, Guy stopped, took out a cigarette, leaned against the wall, and just looked at Mac and Watkins. And smiled.

Watkins shook his head, turned around, stepped inside and ordered the elevator. Seems he figured that Guy would follow him in when it arrived, which he did.

"You ought to give those things up. Those things will kill you. Or at least slow you down if you need to chase some killer down a long alley." With that, Watkins smiled, and Guy figured that he liked to give people trouble too.

Guy stomped out the cigarette before he got on the elevator. *"Yeah, Jack. I may have some bad habits like smoking, occasional drinking, but somehow, I still seem to get the job done."* And decided to give this guy some trouble too, *"When are you going to make Detective, Jack? When you help solve your first crime?"*

Watkins' smile vanished. Guy figured him out correctly. This Detroit Officer had been on the force probably a dozen years, but just didn't seem to have what it takes to solve murders. His strength was in ordering people around, remembering what forensics needed to do, what witnesses to line up, etc. But he couldn't seem to pull it all together and make it make sense. Not like Guy. Guy had always been the best, even though it wasn't in this city. It would take time for them to learn what he could do. And now he had made his first partner here hate him. He sighed, because it made him regret the bad start with Watkins. Oh, well, he could change that, given the time.

As the elevator doors opened, they could hear Sergeant Rick Wylie yelling at everybody, and occasionally shouting Jack's name. Both men took deep breaths and stepped out into the hallway, heading towards the voice. This they both were used to.

Sergeant Wylie stood in the middle of what you could call the main living room of the victim's apartment, on the 12th floor. It was still late afternoon, but Guy felt like going to a motel and either collapsing or finding the bar. He was really feeling that long drive and realizing he shouldn't have driven here through the night. He had been awake for over 36 hours and knew he would be for another 8 at least.

What he hated the most were the smells. There was a smell to homicidal death. Some of it was blood, some was the seared skin around the wounds, some was fingerprint powders, and forensic chemicals. It was unlike any other mixture of scents. And it stayed with you, kind of like an aftertaste of a drink. Oh, how Guy wished he had a drink right then.

He tried to concentrate on the crime scene. He felt he might be able to tell what kind of a personality this victim had by the way his apartment was decorated. Cold. Sterile. Unemotional and unfeeling. Probably a people user.

The apartment was painted stark white, the floor all through the rooms was tiled in black and white. The furniture was avantgarde, black and white. The victim was a professional fashion photographer, and the walls reflected his work. Mostly black and white prints of females. All kinds of gorgeous females. That part, Guy appreciated. Some of the pictures were of various parts of the female anatomy, like one was of a breast, just some girl's breast. Black and white. Guy studied that one for quite awhile. It reminded him of her, then he could picture her red hair in his mind again. He shook his head to clear it.

Everyone was done, or mostly gone. Forensics was gone. Coroner's officers were gone. So was the body. The body had been a mess apparently, judging by the huge red blobs left behind. Guy got out his notebook. He always liked to write down his first impressions of a crime scene. Not that he needed to remind himself, just because he got feelings from it. Impressions.

The impression he got from this scene was an old story – that the guy either had a relationship with his killer or had just ended one. And the killer probably did it as sexual revenge. Why? Because the guy was shot in the groin as well as in the heart. From close range. Wylie was in the midst of filling them in as Guy's mind began to wander, as it often did.

The killer could have been a female. Unless it was a guy and he wanted the police to be thrown off by shooting the photographer in the groin. Or the victim was gay and his lover shot him. Damn, but Guy hated cities like this sometimes. There were so many types of people, so many kinds from so many places all over the world, that anything went. Anybody or anything goes. That's cities like New York and Detroit for you.

Guy looked around the room, at the splashed patches of bright red by the bar. In front of the bar, behind the bar, below the bar on the floor. Obviously, that was where the guy was shot. The red was quite an accent, against all the black and white. When the guy was alive, he should have used red accents, it looked better.

Guy looked at his notes again. He had written down everything that Wylie had told them. Victim was Victor Valentine, approximately 45-50 years of age, fashion photographer, originally from England. Three years in Detroit. Lived here exclusively, according to the landlord and the bills they found in his desk. They had this guy's life, right here in the desk. Guy moved over to the desk and picked up the appointment book. This was where Guy would start his part of the investigation. He figured that he was pulled into this on a lark, so he would deliver as he always did.

As he looked back through the past few days' notations, he realized how much of a perfectionist this guy was. He made notes on everything. Usually, Guy didn't have so much to work with. Maybe this murder would be solved this week. Maybe even today, as he looked at his watch. It was now dinner time. And somehow his stomach had decided to join in that silent conversation.

As Guy and Jack ducked under the crime tapes covering the doorway, he looked again at the second set of red stains in the hallway. Guy's impression was that this was someone else's blood. He wouldn't know for sure for a couple of hours yet, but he felt that it may even be the killer's blood. He just couldn't figure out how Valentine could have shot his killer out here, gone back inside to be shot himself and then die without his gun being found anywhere in the apartment. This hallway blood definitely added a twist. Then, there was the heavy bronze statue that was lying near the bar on the floor. There was blood and hair on one end of the base. When he got the report on the blood types and hair samples, he would know more.

When he and Jack were downstairs by the front door, he was surprised to see the officer called Mac still there guarding the crime scene. The man looked at them. Guy knew that he looked about as unlike a professional detective as one could get. Wrinkled clothes, stubble on his face, messed up hair. But, that was his way lately. They could get used to it, like they were trying to back in New York.

He didn't have any plans to look like a stockbroker from Wall Street. There were enough of those guys in police departments already. And he had been one of them, until about a year ago. Today, he does his *'own thing'* and they could just accept that.

When they got back in his car, he wished he could take another swig. He knew he still had a long night ahead, after a long day and night yesterday. Maybe he should think about taking some more time off after he finished in Detroit. A guy could grow old fast in this job.

CHAPTER 3

THE GIRL

Ralph first noticed the girl when she was standing at the ticket counter. She looked like she was either going to pass out or get sick. He hoped she was buying a ticket for another bus driver's route, not his. He got is double-sized cup of heart-burn coffee from the machine and headed out to do the final check on his bus. Even though someone else was supposed to do the maintenance checks on his bus, he always liked to check out the engine, tires and see if the bathroom had been cleaned. It was his responsibility to keep his riders safe. Mostly, though, it was because of his wife. She was always harping on him to make sure he was going to stay safe and come home to her. He smiled at the thought of how she always stood there with her hands on her hips until satisfied that he was listening to her. They had been married over 20 years and he felt really lucky that she still cared so much about him. His 'little woman.'

Bad news. After he was satisfied the bus was in fairly good condition, he began receiving riders. And there she was. The girl. Up close, she looked worse than he first thought. Her hair was damp and clinging, hanging lifelessly. Her face was pale and her eyes looked almost glazed over. Her outfit looked like she had raided a local second-hand army outlet. She was either on drugs or drunk.

He took her ticket stub and watched her move slowly, rather unsteadily, down the aisle. He hoped she would go in the back, lie down and sleep it off, whatever it was. Then, he became distracted with the next rider handing him her ticket.

When it was time, he sat down in his driver's seat and made his little speech, introducing himself, and reminding the riders of their route, just in case they were on the wrong bus. *"Next stop is Toledo, Ohio."* He was looking at everyone through his mirror, as he maneuvered out into the traffic, heading South on I-95. He could see the girl, way in back, then watched as she disappeared, apparently lying down. Good. Now, he could concentrate on his driving.

He was the company's most popular driver at Tri-City Bus Company. They had rewarded.him for his friendliness and his concern for his riders with a fat raise every year. He was happy in his job and liked to watch and read people. That's why he was so concerned about this girl. He didn't like what he was reading in her. He hated to see young people high on drugs or drink. There was so much more to enjoy in life. And here they were, so young, already screwing up their lives. Well, let them do it somewhere else. Not on his bus.

It was about an hour later when it happened. Some older woman who was seated in the back of the bus had decided to use the bathroom, and saw something wrong when she passed the girl. She screamed so loud that Ralph jumped and almost swerved the bus into another lane of cars. He signaled and pulled over where there was a large enough shoulder near a ramp. He called in on his radio to the dispatcher that he was having trouble and to keep the line cleared for a possible emergency.

When he saw the girl, he knew it was an emergency and hurried to call the dispatcher, swearing all the way back to his radio. *"Got an emergency here. We have a young lady, unconscious and bleeding heavily. We need an ambulance. We are about three miles north of Milltown near the exit ramp. Should I get off and drive her to the hospital in Milltown?"* They told him to stay where he was and wait.

Apparently, there was a police patrol car nearby, because there were two policemen on the bus asking questions within ten minutes. Nobody knew the girl. There was no identification on her. Not even a purse. She just had a few dollars in one of her pockets. Ralph knew he wouldn't forget this one. He shouldn't have let her on the bus to begin with. Now they were going to be late getting back on their main route, which meant his whole schedule was going to be off. His wife would really worry. He decided to send a message to her as soon as they got to Milltown. The dispatcher was sending another bus to get his passengers back on the road. His bus was grounded, the police were going to take it. It was going to be a long night.

Milltown Police Sergeant Gerard Goodwin was on his third cup of coffee when he got a chance to talk to the doctors at Milltown Memorial. The girl had gone through some surgery for a gunshot wound to her left shoulder. The doctors didn't think the wound was any real problem. The bullet had made a clean hole, entrance and exit were both easy to stitch and should heal with no problems. The bullet just missed the shoulder bone, the pathway being about the best location with minimal damage. She was lucky. What the doctors were concerned about was the bruise behind her right ear, which had caused her brain to swell. There didn't appear to be a blood clot in the area, but she was still unconscious, and it was from more than the loss of blood. They would all have to wait until she woke up to see what kind of brain damage there might be.

There was no bullet for evidence, so Goodwin collected the labels from her clothing, got her fingerprints, and headed back to his office. He wanted to check the missing persons reports in the area surrounding Detroit first, then go wider if nothing showed up. If they couldn't find anything about who she was, then it was protocol to contact the local FBI office.

She had to come from somewhere, and she must have someone who had noticed her missing. Actually, judging from her outward appearance and the fact that she had no purse, she could have been a victim of a crime in the city, before she boarded the bus. And, in a big city like Detroit, it was easy to become a nonperson. It was a perfect place to get lost if you wanted to. If she was a runaway, though, there should be a missing report on her somewhere. He crossed his fingers as he sat down to the computer.

Milltown may be a small town, on a bus route between large cities, but there was a lot to be said about small towns. Everybody knew everybody. And they all helped each other out when needed. It was the only way towns in this country used to be, before people started fighting so hard to just survive. Sgt. Goodwin had been around for over 30 years and was sad the way so many people had to struggle to feed their families in today's rough economy. So many people have lost the really important values of life. That's why he settled in this town, after five years on the force in New York City. This was where he married and raised his family. Their values were still intact.

He thought about this young girl's parents and how they must be worried about her, especially being in such a violent place as Detroit. You couldn't pay Goodwin to let any of his kids or grandkids live in the city. They all lived within a mile of one another in Milltown. A great little town.

A few hours later, he had to face the fact that there was no one matching this girl's description that was missing. The ones that sounded like possibilities didn't check out once the pictures were sent to him. There was no match for the fingerprints either. Goodwin decided to call the hospital and check on the girl's condition. Maybe she had woken up and would be able to tell him something. So, he crossed his fingers and picked up the phone. As he waited to talk with the doctor in charge of her case, he looked at his fingers. He didn't remember where he had picked up that habit…of crossing his fingers before doing something. Maybe it came from his grandfather. He vaguely recalled seeing him do it a few times. But his grandfather, whom he had adored, died when Goodwin was only ten years old. And, funny thing, he still thought about him today. Probably because he had spent so much time with his grandfather those first few years. Until some braindead dopehead took that great man away from his loving family. Another reason why Goodwin hated New York City.

Well, the girl was still unconscious, and the doctor was sure it was from the head wound. As Goodwin hung up the phone, he decided to go home and get a couple of hours sleep. Then, he would check in the morning to see if she came out of the coma. He hoped so. This whole thing was giving him a bad feeling. Maybe because she reminded him of his daughter a little. Same age. Same innocent young face when she was sleeping. Still innocent in a lot of ways.

CHAPTER 4

ON THE CASE

Detective and Profiler Guy Davis found a spare desk at headquarters in Detroit around 9am. After being awake for two days, he had caught five hours of sleep, showered and shaved. Even though his body was at rest for those five hours, his mind had continued milling through the events of the last couple of days. He didn't feel any closer to answers on this case but knew what he had to do next.

Sergeant Rick Wylie was surprised and impressed to see Davis when he got to headquarters. He was still standing next to his desk when he saw Officer Jack Watkins arrive and have the same reaction. They nodded to one another, and Watkins walked over to Davis. Not many could keep those crazy hours that they did and still be able to function. He asked Davis, *"You get any sleep last night in that seedy motel you stayed at?"*

Guy Davis stood to answer the question, a good chance to stretch, which he did, *"A few hours. Bad back on a bad bed, so you might just see me do a lot of this today."* And he stretched again.

The booming voice of Chief Bill Overton cut through the almost quiet of the room. *"Davis and Watkins. Here. Now."*

Watkins smiled and winked, as they turned to go and see the Chief.

"Sit. So, the case we were having so much trouble solving when we called New York to get you here? Well, we don't need

you now. We have solved that case. It was the Mayor, and we got enough evidence to hang the bastard. You can go back home if you want to, Davis."

Guy Davis sat in the chair, looked over at Watkins, "Actually, sir, I would like to stay and see this new case through. Since Jack needed a partner and we seem to be able to work together pretty well," Jack nodded in agreement, "I think I can be of some help. Why arrive one day, then leave the next? It takes longer than that just to drive here."

The Chief sat and mulled this over a bit, "Watkins, what do you think?"

There was a trace of a smile on Jack's face, "Chief, I really could use the help. And I've never worked with a Detective who is a Profiler too. I would like that experience."

The Chief sighed, as he picked up a file in front of him, "Well, okay. Let's give it a few days. But report to me at the end of each day, okay?"

Without waiting for an answer, he opened the file and brought it up to his face to read. Guy wondered, 'Bad eyesight, or a signal for us to leave?'

Watkins stood up and turned to the door, and Guy followed him. Jack turned around, walking backwards, "Let's grab some breakfast down the street while we discuss the case." Then turned, went to his desk, grabbed his jacket, and walked out, expecting Guy to simply follow him. Which he did.

As they ordered at Watkins' favorite greasy spoon down the street, Guy appraised his new partner. Neat dresser, dirty blonde hair fashionably cut, handsome facial features, nice smile and bright blue eyes, even after working these long, grueling hours. Jack looked athletic, with muscles that looked like he worked out a lot. Guy couldn't figure when the guy would find time.

"Okay, I've got some ideas, but I'd like to hear your impressions, Jack."

Watkins wasn't sure how to take this new guy in town, who just seemed to jump in and take over their case discussion like that. Well, he did have to work with the guy, so he took a breath and pulled his notebook out from his jacket pocket, putting it on the table but not opening it. He began recalling details from memory so he could start drawing some conclusions to share with Davis. *"Valentine was obviously killed in front of his bar, due to the blood patches. He was killed by one gunshot wound to the heart. The shot in the groin was an afterthought."* He paused wanting this fact to show Guy that he had already talked with the coroner's office. Guy nodded, so Jack continued, *"Bullets were 38 caliber. No gun found yet, we are still looking. The killer knew Valentine. There were two glasses out, one almost full, the other half-full. No clear fingerprints on either glass. There was a partial print on the lip of the fuller glass. Turned out to be Valentine's. The afterthought shot to the groin could have been emotional, showing sexual revenge of some sort. Or – maybe intentional to throw us off in the wrong direction."*

He paused only for a moment, taking a drink, then, *"That may depend on finding the blood donor from the hallway. I checked the report before you arrived at the station – not Valentine's blood. Same blood was found on the statue as in the hallway. We have a hair sample to make comparisons when the time comes. The blood could belong to the killer, but I doubt it. We recovered a bullet from the wall near the blood stains. A 38 caliber, same as killed Valentine. I think it could have been one of two scenarios. One being the gun used was Valentine's gun and he had shot at the killer in the hallway, who then fought over the gun, won, then shoved Valentine back into the room, shooting him. But we would have found the killer's blood inside the apartment. No sign inside, except on the statue."*

Guy leaned forward, *"So, could be someone saw the killing, a witness. Killer shot at witness, who got away. We found some blood both in the elevator, and on the inside of the apartment building front door. We need someone to check out gunshot wound victims at the area hospitals who also have head wounds. Maybe we'll get lucky. And we still need to check the victim's rented photo studio."*

"*We should do that today.*" Jack pulled out Valentine's appointment book, "*Let's see some people today. Then we can check the studio on the way.*"

Guy finished his coffee, stood, tossed some money on the table, and the two walked out. Guy felt a small smile on his face. He liked the way Watkins' mind worked. The Officer had promise. He could make Detective yet.

Look for "*A Matter of Time*" from the Guy Davis Series, available on Amazon by late 2022.

OTHER BOOKS BY THE AUTHOR

"Beyond, Tales of Life, Mystery & Murder"

Fictional short stories from a nursing home to the Bayou, where something can happen and be a lie, another thing may not happen and seem truer than the truth. Oh, yes, there is also some non-fiction in the book.

Available on Amazon in soft cover and Kindle.

www.MarilynDayton.com

"Beyond 2, Strange But True Short Stories"

A collection of tales based on real life experiences, where the similarities are in how extraordinary the stories are.

Available on Amazon in soft cover and Kindle.

www.MarilynDayton.com

"Reflexions, Lessons Learned Along Life's Journey"

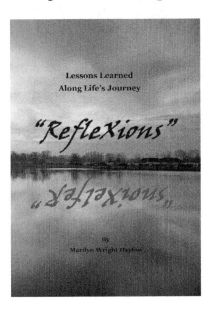

A collection of short stories, from the author's life, based on her blog From Glam 2 Gram. Stories from when she knew a young Elvis Presley, to her mentor Dick Clark, through her various adventures in radio and TV, and life as an entrepreneur.

Available on Amazon in soft cover and Kindle.

www.MarilynDayton.com

"Murder on the Mesa"

A HIGHTOWER MYSTERY, BOOK 1

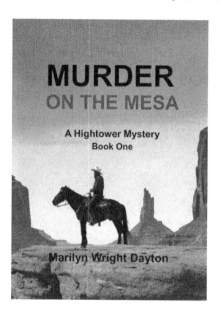

"Think Murder She Wrote, Miss Marple, Hercule Poirot - All Rolled Into One!"

This is 'edge of your seat' reading, with 'engrossing characters'. Solving crime has no age limit. Meet four ladies who are in their 70's, led by Weezie Hightower, retired Private Investigator. Weezie and Guy Davis, retired detective, head across country to Arizona, and solve a murder mystery that has SEVEN suspects. And it only takes them SEVEN days to solve it.

"Heartbreaking But Intriguing!"

Available NOW on Amazon in soft cover and Kindle.

www.MarilynDayton.com

"The Faces of Murder"

A HIGHTOWER MYSTERY, BOOK 2

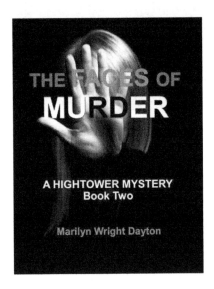

"In the Vein of Murder She Wrote and Miss Marple!"

This is another 'edge of your seat' reading, with 'engrossing characters'. The Cackle Gang is back, led by Weezie Hightower, retired Private Investigator. Weezie and two of the gals head across country on a train from California to NYC, where they need to solve several murders, all while parked in a small town in the middle of nowhere, in the desert. And why does the FBI need to get involved?

Available NOW on Amazon in soft cover and Kindle.

www.MarilynDayton.com

MORE HIGHTOWER MYSTERY SERIES COMING IN 2021 THRU 2025

"Murder on Trial"

A HIGHTOWER MYSTERY, BOOK 3

"You Are My Last Hope."

A young man is on trial for murder. There are almost too many clues…what's the real story? The Hightower gals, known as the Cackle Gang, find the story confusing as they work together to solve the mystery before the verdict that would send him to his death.

COMING IN 2023

www.MarilynDayton.com

"A Question of Murder"

A HIGHTOWER MYSTERY, BOOK 4

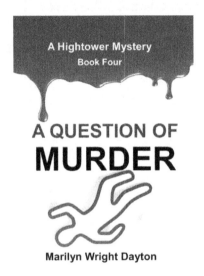

"Was it suicide or murder?"

The case is cold…VERY cold. Jake Hightower joins his aunt to help solve a case she and her late husband had worked on a couple of decades ago. There was always that question…"Was it suicide or murder?" In this riveting mystery, the second question is whether it was the first in a series of murders, and can they disprove the original claim of suicide in this reawakened crime.

COMING IN EARLY 2024

www.MarilynDayton.com

"Murder on High"

A HIGHTOWER MYSTERY, BOOK 5

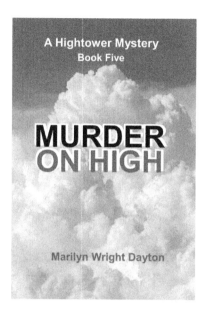

"How could this happen??"

No one expects to find dead bodies on a plane, but that is what happens to Bitsy, and her screams sound even louder up in the clouds. Bitsy and the rest of the Hightower Mysteries gals are taking a small holiday that will not end up as planned. And how does this case relate back to another one in Weezie's P.I. past?

COMING IN 2025

www.MarilynDayton.com

"The Hollow Soul"
A Political Thriller

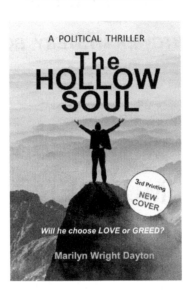

Award-Winning Novel – Selected TOP PICK
By TaleFlick.com

"LOVE or GREED – which one is stronger?"

Joseph Pahana is a man pure of heart and soul who loves the people, and they love him. And he falls in love with beautiful Maya. All seems well, UNTIL…

-   He decides to run for President.
-   He becomes blind to his ambition
-   The politicians turn against him.
    He has everything to gain – and everything to lose.

"Riveting! Engrossing! Intriguing!"

Available NOW on Amazon in soft cover and Kindle.

www.MarilynDayton.com

"A Matter of Time"

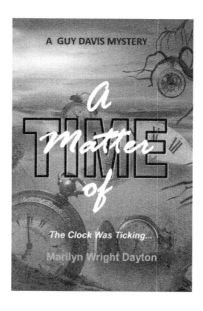

"A Who-Done-It of the Highest Order

Guy Davis starts his own murder mystery stories, in the years before the Hightower Mysteries. He was a detective, who followed the crime, no matter where it was. "**A Matter of Time**" is the first in the Guy Davis Murder Mystery Series.

In Detroit on assignment from his New York City police department, Guy is recovering from a major 'inciting incident' in his private life. He is trying to find his way back to being a productive member of the police force. And it starts in Detroit, where he becomes a temporary detective and profiler in solving a murder mystery. Can he solve it before he runs out of time? He needs to pull himself together and solve the crime. It could just save him.

COMING IN 2022

www.MarilynDayton.com

"Never Say Die"

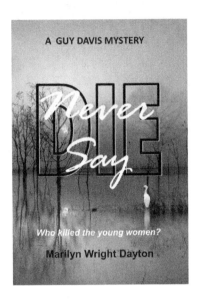

"Another Who-Done-It of the Highest Order

Guy Davis again is living out of his suitcase, another murder mystery story, from the years before the Hightower Mysteries. He was a detective, who followed the crime, no matter where it was. "**Never Say Die**" is the second in the Guy Davis Murder Mystery Series.

In New Orleans, can they find out who has been killing the young women before there is another murder? When you think the case is solved, there is a complication – in the form of another dead young woman. How did that happen? How could their suspect kill another while he was locked up in their jail?

COMING IN 2024

www.MarilynDayton.com

"The Knowing Tree"

Marilyn Wright Dayton

"A Tree Can Talk...Telling Stories?"

"LIFE" goes on all around us and we don't usually think very much about it...in the ground, in the air, in the water, in the plant life. This is the story of one tree - a witness to history, to love, to sorrow, to death. It tell us what "she" witnesses over several centuries - how she watches, how she knows - the life of many under her protective branches, even messages written on her "skin"...

We learn about lives, wars, loves found and lost, family and friends who meet again after decades and witness their changes, but yet how they have stayed the same. We can simply read and enjoy, or we can feel the emotions, full of history, that could change our own lives

COMING IN LATE 2022

www.MarilynDayton.com

"Our Roots Run Deep", the wRightSide Family History

Through many plastic totes of information, the author was able to trace her family directly back to the days of the **Vikings**, through the **Norman Conquest, the War of 1066**, and so much more. Inside this book are included also many historical aspects that show what life was like during each time period. There is even a branch of her family that goes back to **Eric the Forester.** He was the brother of **Eric the Red**, and uncle to **Leif Ericson** (Eric's son) who originally discovered North America.

This book was published in 2020, and is available on Amazon. Everyone should do genealogical research. It opens your eyes to who you really are, and how you became who you are. Fascinating. Find your ancestors. It is an amazing journey, one well worth taking.

www.MarilynDayton.com

www.wrightsidefamily.com

THE OTHER SIDE OF HER MOUNTAIN

Made in the USA
Middletown, DE
03 March 2022

62004894R00036